THE

ADVENTURES

From the makers of Doctor Who

BBC CHILDREN'S BOOKS

Published by the Penguin Group
Penguin Books Ltd, 80 Strand, London WC2R 0RL, England
Penguin Group (USA) Inc., 375 Hudson Street, New York, New York 10014, USA
Penguin Group (Australia) Ltd, 250 Camberwell Road, Camberwell, Victoria, 3124, Australia
(a division of Pearson Australia Group Pty Ltd)
Canada, India, New Zealand, South Africa

Published by BBC Children's Character Books, 2008
Text and design © Children's Character Books, 2008

10 9 8 7 6 5 4 3 2 1

Sarah Jane Adventures © BBC 2007

www.thesja.com

ISBN: 978 1 40590510 7

Printed in Great Britain by Clays Ltd, St Ives plc

THE

ADVENTURES

From the makers of Doctor Who
Series created by Russell T Davies

Day of the Clown

Written by Phil Ford

Based on the script by Phil Ford

'I saw amazing things, out there in space. But there's strangeness to be found wherever you turn. Life on Earth can be an adventure, too.

You just have to know where to look.'

SARAH JANE SMITH

Chapter One

Monday morning news

'There are worse things than aliens,' said Sarah Jane Smith as she tossed the morning's newspaper onto the kitchen table. The front page glared at her...

THIRD CHILD GOES MISSING.

Sarah Jane had been a journalist practically all her adult life and she had been dealing with aliens – good and bad – for almost just as long, but there were some headlines she had never got used to, and there were things that humans did to each other that sometimes made them worse than anything else in the galaxy.

Three children had gone missing in the Ealing area in less than two weeks. The latest, according to the newspaper, was a 14-year-old boy called Tony Warner. He'd been playing football with his mates in the park when the ball had been kicked into a patch of bushes and trees. Tony had gone in to find the ball and had never come out.

As with the others, there was no trace of him. The police, it seemed, had next to nothing to go on. But Sarah Jane hoped they would catch whoever was responsible before another child disappeared, and she prayed that the two boys and girl whose pictures were now in the morning paper would be found safe and well.

Her eyes fell on the tall dark-haired boy at her kitchen table and she felt her heart beat faster at the thought of anything happening to her son. Not that he couldn't take care of himself. He may have been just a boy, but Luke had faced some nasty situations in his short life – he had, in fact, saved the world more than once. He, Sarah Jane, Clyde Langer, and Maria Jackson. Only Maria was gone now. And Luke missed her.

Maria and her dad, Alan, had moved in across Bannerman Road from Sarah Jane a little less than a year ago. In those days there had been no Luke, and Sarah Jane lived alone and got on with her life and the strange things that she did, and no one knew or even cared much about her. To her neighbours Sarah Jane was the slightly odd woman who lived in the big house, spared barely a smile for them, and seemed to be constantly rushing all over the place in her funny little car, or burning the midnight oil up in her attic. And then Maria had seen an alien in Sarah Jane's garden. And everything had started to change.

That was when Bubbleshock was sweeping the country – a sickly sweet drink that was actually part of an invasion plan by an alien race called the Bane. As part of their strategy to turn humans into slaves and food they had also grown the perfect human being from synthesized DNA, and that had been Luke – who Maria and Sarah Jane had helped escape the clutches of the evil Bane leader, Mrs Wormwood.

Luke had been born with the body of a young teenager and the mind of a genius, but when he escaped from the Bane's headquarters he was only a matter of hours old. He could speak and read, he was instinctively brilliant, but he didn't have a clue about the world that he now found himself in. Sarah Jane adopted him (with a little help from the alien supercomputer she kept in her attic called Mr Smith) and had since brought him up as her own. It hadn't always been easy for Luke to find his place in this strange world, sometimes his intelligence made it all the more difficult, but he had come on a long way. Friends like Maria and Clyde – who had later earned his place in the gang with cold chip sandwiches that had exposed the weakness of another alien, the Slitheen – had helped Luke more than Sarah Jane ever could. But, as with even those of us who were born with a belly button, there were still times when something new shook your world.

Four weeks ago Maria had left Bannerman Road with her dad for a new life in America. Maria was special to Luke in a way that not many people would understand – she was the one who had found him in the Bane's Bubbleshock factory, and she was the first person he ever spoke to.

Now he sat at the kitchen table reading an email from her on his laptop computer. She had been keeping in touch since she left, but Sarah Jane could see that he was missing her badly. He hadn't glanced up from the email when she came in with the paper. And she knew he had read it at least three times before.

Sarah Jane poured herself tea from the yellow pot standing on the work surface and tried to put some lightness into her voice, despite her worry for him. 'How is she? Does she like Washington?'

Luke still didn't look up. Sarah Jane noticed that his cereal had been barely touched.

'She says it's awesome,' he told her.

Awesome? How American.

'It sounds like Maria's going to fit in perfectly,' she said, and took her cup of tea to the table and sat down, facing Luke. It was time to talk about this.

'I know it's hard when a really good friend – someone you really care about – moves out of your life, Luke, but you'll see Maria again. She's going to come back for her mum's wedding, isn't she? I'm sure we'll all meet up then.'

Sarah Jane had always suspected that there was still a torch burning between Maria's estranged parents, Alan and Chrissie, but news of the new job in Washington and their decision to go had obviously blown out any last hopes of them getting back together. As Maria and Alan had said their goodbyes on Bannerman Road, Chrissie had told them that she was going to marry her boyfriend Ivan. Maria and Alan had welcomed the news. It was, perhaps, the new start that the family had always needed. But the parting of families had always saddened Sarah Jane – it was the legacy of her own tragic family history, she supposed.

But Luke wasn't convinced by Sarah Jane's comforting. Maria's return for the wedding wouldn't be the same, he said. She might be there for a week, and then she would be gone again.

'It won't be the same. It never will be.'

Sarah Jane ached for his hurting, and reached out and took his hand: 'Maybe not, but, you know, that's not always so bad. One of the best things about life is that it's always surprising us.'

And that was when Clyde Langer bounded through the back door, school bag over his shoulder.

'Morning people,' he beamed – Clyde always beamed, even sometimes when he was being chased by an alien intent on eating him. He grabbed a piece of toast lying untouched by Luke. 'This is Clyde Langer reporting live from Bannerman Road where, at this precise moment, a new family is moving in at Number thirty-six.'

He took a bite out of the toast and grinned,

'Come see!'

Outside, Sarah Jane saw a removal truck parked outside the house that used to belong to Maria and Alan Jackson. There was no sign of the new family, but a squad of thick-chested removal men were hefting furniture along the path and through the front door.

Clyde shook his head as he finished off the toast. 'Boy, they have no idea what they're moving in over the road from!'

Sarah Jane whirled on him, 'No! And they're never going to find out, do you hear?'

Luke was joining them now; he had grabbed his school bag and was slipping it over his shoulder as he reached the bottom of the drive.

'Both of you,' she said, 'promise me you'll never breathe a word about what we do, Mr Smith, any of it.'

Maria finding out about the aliens had been an accident. The arrivals of Luke and Clyde had, in their way, been a result of that accident. Looking back now, Sarah Jane wouldn't have wanted it any other way, but in the old days she didn't have to worry about anyone apart from herself. She didn't need history repeating itself, and she didn't need someone else to watch out for.

The arrival of a new family in Maria's old house had done nothing for Luke's mood.

'Why would we say anything,' he said. 'It's not like it's Maria, is it? Come on, Clyde. We're going to be late.'

And Sarah Jane's heart broke a little as she watched Luke begin to head off up the road. Clyde exchanged a glance with Sarah Jane. He missed Maria, too, but not like Luke.

'Don't worry,' he told Sarah Jane, 'he'll be all right. And we won't say anything about what goes off over here. That's for Our Eyes Only. We'd just better hope Maria never left anything lying around over there when she moved.'

'What do you mean?'

Clyde shrugged, like it was obvious: 'Well, we've been hanging with some pretty random intergalactic sorts. Who knows what might have rubbed off and dropped off over there?'

And Clyde hurried off to catch up with Luke, leaving Sarah Jane watching the removal men carrying things into Maria's old house, and worrying about what might lurk there, waiting for the new owners.

Chapter Two

Rani

Monday morning at Park Vale School. Just the same as any Monday morning. A thousand kids making a lot of noise about what they'd done over the weekend, and about how they so did not want to be here today. Among them, Clyde and Luke were heading for their lockers, and Luke was on the defensive.

'I did not fancy Maria!'

But Clyde was grinning; Luke couldn't lie to him and get away with it. Clyde prided himself on having played a significant part in Luke's development as a human being, and that was mainly down to 'Clyde's Cool Rules'.

'Boy I taught you well, didn't I? Clyde's Cool Rule Number Two – deny all emotion, especially where involving girls.'

But Luke was defiant. 'I just miss her, okay? Don't you?'

Clyde had to admit, he had a point there.

'Course I miss her. But people move on, Luke. Ask my mum and dad.'

Clyde's dad had run out on him and his mum when he was five years old to live with Melba – his dad's sister-in-law. Clyde knew all about losing someone: he hadn't laid eyes on his dad since and he never wanted to.

'I've never lost anyone before,' Luke said.

And he might have only been five years old, but Clyde could remember like it was yesterday how that felt.

'It's not going to be the same without her, that's for sure,' Clyde said, and felt the old emotions coming up from the place where he had them locked away.

He slammed the lid down on his feelings with Cool Rule Two. 'I mean, who am I going to have to save from Sontarans, the Slitheen and Gorgons, now?'

And as he pulled a bunch of books out of his locker and turned back to Luke he was almost knocked over from behind.

'Hey,' he snapped. 'Watch where you're –'

Only Clyde kind of forgot what he was going to say. The girl that had almost knocked him over, and was now collecting her books off the floor, was quite a looker. As she stood up, he saw that she was tall and slender, with deep dark eyes. Just for a moment the Cool Rules were forgotten.

The girl flashed a slightly nervous smile, 'Sorry. I'm looking for Mr Cunningham's form.'

'That's our class.'

Clyde heard Luke talking. He seemed to have momentarily lost the ability to speak, himself. She was new. A new girl on the block. And she was in their form. Clyde liked Mondays.

'I start today,' the girl said.

'And you run into me. That's what I call a start,' Clyde beamed, glad that he'd recovered the power of speech with such a stunning line.

The girl gave him a wry smile. 'Yeah, like starting the hundred metres in the Olympics and tripping over your laces!'

Had she chucked a bucket of water over Clyde, it couldn't have been more effective – but at least it put a smile on Luke's face.

'This is Clyde. He thinks he's cool. I'm Luke.'

'Who isn't?'

The girl smiled, a little more relaxed, 'I'm Rani.

My family just moved in to Bannerman Road.'

Bannerman Road?

And Clyde looked at Luke. 'Of course. Where else? Sarah Jane is right, the universe never stops weirding you out!'

'Sarah who?' asked Rani.

'Never mind,' Luke told her. 'Come on, we'll take you to class. It's this way.'

But as they moved off, Rani froze; her eyes locked for a moment somewhere off down the corridor.

'Hey, are you all right?' Clyde asked.

'Did you see that?' she asked, her eyes flashing from whatever had been along the corridor to Clyde.

'See what?' All he could see were dozens of kids putting off the inevitable of having to go to class.

But Rani shook her head, dismissing the subject. 'Never mind. Come on. I'd better not be late.'

She flashed Clyde another smile, but he could see the nerves behind it again.

Well, first day at school. Meeting Clyde Langer. Who wouldn't have nerves?

And by the time they reached the door to their form room Clyde had forgotten all about whatever Rani thought she had seen.

Rani hadn't though, although she tried.

But the business of settling in at a new school at least gave her some distraction. And Luke and Clyde seemed nice enough. Their form teacher was all right, too. Mr Cunningham was in his late thirties, a broad man with thinning hair and a big smile. As Rani sat with Luke and Clyde Mr Cunningham took the form through the day's notes – the school football team was out of the Inter-School Challenge Cup after a mauling by one of the other local comprehensives. It was news that the form took with a chorus of good-natured boos and hisses. But he was hoping for better success in the science competition that was coming up...

'Anyone who wants to sign up for the team should see Miss Webster,' he told the class. 'Luke Smith, I'll be expecting to see your name on the list.'

And the class made their views known on that chanting, Lukey! Lukey! Lukey!

Rani was impressed, 'You a bit of a brain-box then, Luke?'

Luke shrugged uneasily. He was smiling, but uncomfortable with the attention.

'They haven't got a box big enough,' Clyde told her.

But Luke's raucous fan-base was abruptly cut silent by a command from the back of the classroom.

'That's enough! Silence, the lot of you!'

Every head in there turned – even Mr Cunningham's.

Framed in the doorway was an athletic dark-haired man in his early forties. And he needn't have said anything, just one look told them all that he was hard as nails. His suit was perfectly pressed, without a crease, his shirt shone white against his dark skin, and his tie was pulled into a tight knot that looked so symmetrical you got the feeling he may have calculated the angles as he tied it.

'This is a classroom,' he barked as he made his way towards Mr Cunningham, 'not the home end at Stamford Bridge!'

At the front of the class, Mr Cunningham looked only a shade less stunned than the rest of them. 'Class, this is Mr Chandra. Our new Head.'

Whoops!

And every eye was trained on the new Head Teacher as he moved around the room. He moved like a cat. No, a panther.

'So let's get one thing straight from Day One,' Mr Chandra told them, his voice now quieter, but laced with threat, 'this is a school. You come here to learn, not to play about.'

And Mr Chandra, the panther, leaped on a boy a couple of seats down from Luke, who sat slumped in his seat doodling on the cover of an exercise book. 'You boy! Sit up straight and pay attention!'

The boy jumped straight. Luke jumped, too.

Clyde exchanged a look with Rani. He thought she looked almost terrified.

'Now,' Mr Chandra continued, as he joined Mr Cunningham, 'it's been a while since your last Head Teacher, Mr Blakeman, disappeared.'

Oh boy, thought Clyde, if only this guy knew the truth about that it would knock the chip off his shoulder. Blakeman had been a Slitheen, part of a family of inter-galactic chancers that was set on robbing Earth of all its energy – including the sun.

'It seems that some of the school's standards vanished with him,' Mr Chandra snapped, favouring Mr Cunningham with a withering look. 'But, listen up! Park Vale has a new captain on the bridge now.'

Clyde leaned across to Rani, 'Oh, no. I'm getting a very serious sinking feeling.'

And he saw Rani roll her eyes with disbelief as she watched the man at the front of the class.

'I'm a fair captain,' he was saying, 'but believe me, I run a tight ship. And I expect every one of you on course for the same destination – top marks. Not just the exams. Every piece of work you do. And any slackers will answer to me!'

'Aye aye, skipper!' And Clyde had said it before he could stop himself.

There was a murmur of laughter among the other kids, and Mr Chandra homed in on Clyde like a missile. 'The joker in the pack!'

'I do my best,' Clyde smiled back and wondered, did he really think this was going to win this guy over?

Mr Chandra grabbed the exercise book lying before Clyde and checked the name. 'Well, Clyde Langer, I hope your classwork is as sharp as your wit.'

And Clyde knew he was just in too deep now to pull back. 'Don't worry sir. It takes brains to be this funny.'

Rani saw Mr Chandra's face darken like an ocean storm – and then she saw something else.

The clown at the window behind him.

But that was impossible. They had come up the

stairs to the form room. It was on the first floor.

But there was a clown outside the window, a white-faced clown with points of ginger hair and a big red mouth, dressed in a costume of red, yellow and blue and he was looking straight at her. And he was holding a red balloon on a string in one gloved hand. And she just knew that he had that balloon especially for her. And he couldn't possibly be there. Because there was nothing he could be standing on out there.

Her eyes flashed around the room. No one else could see the clown. But still he was there, offering her the balloon. Just as he had been earlier, for that fleeting moment in the school corridor. She had seen him standing among the bustling crowd of school kids that had moved around him, had for all she knew, moved through him.

This couldn't be happening, she told herself.

The Head Teacher tossed Clyde's exercise book back on to the table before him.

'No, Langer. It takes brains to know when to shut up and listen!'

And the clown had gone.

Rani sat back in her chair, trying to make some sense of her thoughts, trying to work out what was happening to her.

At the front of the class, Mr Chandra had pushed his hands into his pockets as he ploughed on. 'Now, a third child has gone missing. I'm speaking to all classes today, reminding you all to be careful and – just as importantly – telling you all that if you see anything or anyone suspicious, tell the police immediately.'

Rani's eyes found the window again. Yeah, maybe she should tell the police, should tell someone, but – let's face it – who on earth was going to believe her?

Chapter Three

Do you save the world every day?

Sarah Jane felt wrong. This was not her, at all. She stood on the doorstep of the house that had until recently been Maria's home. In one hand she held a vacuum flask filled with tea, in the other she held a plate of cakes. Nothing could have been more alien for Sarah Jane.

She pressed the doorbell and waited for her new neighbour to show herself. Sarah Jane had waited for the removal men to finish work, and then she had given her new neighbour another hour to open boxes, find the first broken china,

8 F T Y 3 B N A 1 K L D 6 R E 9 S X 5 P O C Z **19**

realise that the couch was never going to fit in the lounge and that her favourite CDs had mysteriously never made it from the last house to this one. Then Sarah Jane had been unable to wait any longer. If Clyde was right, and that maybe something extra-terrestrial had somehow made it back to Maria's house, she had to find it and deal with it quickly. It was possible. After all, Sarah Jane had herself once unwittingly carried a plague of Squaleen locusts home with her after visiting a Prastaki trading ship from the Thunderhead Spiral Galaxy. Squaleen locusts are almost microscopic but they have enormous appetites and seem to love the taste of furniture stuffing. They also reproduce every fifteen minutes. Sarah Jane had to completely refurnish her house by the time she had dealt with them.

When no one answered the doorbell, Sarah Jane felt a chill creep through her bones – what if something worse than Squaleen locusts had been waiting here?

Sarah Jane pressed the doorbell again, and this time the door opened. Behind it stood a woman in her late thirties dressed in jeans, tee-shirt and yellow rubber gloves. She looked grimy and hassled.

'Yes? Hello?' she asked.

'Hello,' Sarah Jane began, struggling to look like a good neighbour. 'I live over the road. I saw you were moving in. Thought maybe you haven't been able to find the kettle yet.'

And the woman's eyes settled on the flask and cakes and her face lit up. 'Oh, tell me, do you save the world every day, or is it just on Mondays?'

Sarah Jane found she could only smile.

And her new neighbour was smiling, too, 'Come in, come in.'

Sarah Jane stepped over the threshold and followed the woman between the piles of boxes into the lounge as she apologized for the mess.

'Sorry it's such a state,' she said. 'I had a plan – a list of what was what and where it was going. But then you have to go and use removal men, don't you? Forget it, you might as well give in to chaos. I'm Gita.'

Gita offered her hand, and Sarah Jane juggled the cakes and flask to take it.

'Sarah Jane.'

Gita beamed: 'Well, it's very nice to meet you, Sarah.'

'Jane.'

'Lovely.'

And Gita went off to find some cups, as Sarah Jane laid down the flask and cakes and flicked back the face of her wristwatch and began to scan the room with the alien technology embedded in the watch body. All life gives off energy. Scientists had even photographed the energy that humans radiated. They called it kirlean energy. Aliens were no different, but every species had its individual energy which left traces wherever they went. As Sarah Jane scanned, Gita hunted through boxes in the kitchen for cups.

'This has been a nightmare, I can't tell you. We should have moved in last Friday but the removal company double-booked us. Can you believe it?'

'Oh, no,' Sarah Jane called back, all her concentration on the scanner on her wrist.

'So, that's your house over the road, is it, Sarah?'

'Sarah Jane,' she muttered, eyes still on the scanner.

'The big one, right opposite. Have you got kids?'

The scan was negative. Sarah Jane closed her watch with a smile. 'All clear.'

As Gita showed up with two mugs, 'Sorry?'

'A son,' Sarah Jane said quickly. 'Luke. There's just the two of us.'

Gita glowed. 'We've got a girl. Rani. She's fifteen.

Very clever. Shall I be mother?'

Without waiting for an answer, Gita opened the flask and started to pour. Sarah Jane could see that Gita was the kind of woman who got on with things. She couldn't have been any more different to Chrissie Jackson. Though, she supposed, the world did owe quite a debt to Maria's mum and the designer high heels that she had so often tottered around Bannerman Road in. She had, in fact, saved the world with one. The universe, Sarah Jane reminded herself, was a place of constant surprise.

'So what do you do for a living, Sarah?' Gita asked as she handed her one of the mugs.

What was it with the women in this house? None of them could get her name right. Was it that difficult? But she decided to let it go.

'I'm a freelance journalist.'

Gita's face lit up with interest and delight. 'A journalist? My Rani wants to be a journalist. What a coincidence! Maybe she could come round? You could give her some tips.'

Yes! Marvellous! Just what she wanted!

'Oh. Well, my work tends to be rather specialised,' Sarah Jane told Gita, and tried to sweeten the dismissal with a smile. 'And I am really very busy.'

But Gita wasn't the sort of woman to let a dismissal put her off. She continued to beam like a searchlight. 'Rani will be so excited. And she and your Luke are bound to be friends. You'll love her. She's very curious. Wants to know everything about everybody.'

Sarah Jane felt her smile sag with dread – that was all she needed. A nosy fifteen-year-old neighbour. Sometimes the universe was surprising, and sometimes it seemed that it just had it in for you.

Chapter Four

Weird

Rani had managed to get through her first morning at Park Vale without seeing any more clowns. As she walked across the playground with Luke life felt almost normal. A little way off, Clyde was playing basketball with some mates and she did her best to ignore him as he tried to show off for her. It wasn't all that difficult, and it was kinder that way – Clyde wasn't actually much of a basketball player. Even if he was kind of cute, in his own way.

She couldn't help wondering what kind of common ground he and Luke found to be friends, but it was pretty obvious that the two of them were best mates. Perhaps Luke had been bullied in the past, she thought, and Clyde had looked after him. That would make sense, she thought. Luke

8FTY3BNA1KLD6RE9SX5POCZ **25**

was the kind of thoughtful kid that would get picked on and Clyde, for all his show of rebellion, was the kind of guy that would stick up for other people. She felt glad to have fallen in with the two of them.

'So what were the last people like that lived in our house,' she asked Luke as they crossed the playground and, behind them, Clyde called for the basketball. 'Mr Jackson and his daughter?'

'Nice,' said Luke. 'I miss Maria.'

Rani grinned, 'Oh yes?'

Luke was quickly on the defensive. 'We were friends. Maria, Clyde and me.'

'We can be friends.'

Luke glanced away. 'Yes. But it wouldn't be the same.'

'Oh. Sorry I suggested it.'

Luke turned, his eyes wide with apology. 'No – I didn't mean. I can't explain...'

His embarrassment was comical, Rani almost laughed.

'It's all right, Luke.'

He shrugged, 'Interpersonal-relationships are something I haven't mastered yet.'

'You know, Luke, I hope you don't mind me telling you – but you do know you're a bit weird, don't you? I mean, I think you're all right. Just a bit strange.'

It sounded like it wasn't news to him. 'I'm not strange, I'm just different. There's a difference.'

Like she said, weird.

But not the weirdest thing around here. Those kids going missing, she told him that was weird. And the police just didn't have a clue.

Luke tried to reassure her. He told her that statistically the chances of her being abducted were extremely remote.

She looked at him like he'd just proven everything that she had said. 'Like I said, strange. I'm not worried, Luke, I'm interested. That's all. It's weird.' And she thought uneasily of the clown, his face pressed to the first floor window, a red balloon in his hand, 'I'm into weird.'

Luke watched her, thought about telling her that she had moved into the right road, then. Behind them, Clyde scored a basket and looked hopefully to see if Rani had noticed, but she had other things on her mind.

'Have you ever seen anything strange?' she asked Luke. 'I mean, around school.'

Luke wondered what she was getting at, but that was when Clyde tried to repeat his basket just as the new Head passed by, and instead he hit Mr Chandra on the back of his head with the ball.

The Head's bark silenced the playground. 'Langer! My office! Now!'

And so, an hour later, Clyde was sitting outside Mr Chandra's office, where the Head Teacher had left him since angrily escorting him up the stairs, telling Clyde that he was really going to have to sort his act out if the two of them were going to get along. Mr Chandra wasn't at all interested in Clyde's apologies and assurances that it had been an accident. Looking on the bright side, as he watched the hands creep around their circuit of the clock face, Clyde had to admit that his punishment could have been worse.

'Are you still here?'

It was Dave Finn. He was a tall, skinny kid. Unlike Clyde, he was a natural for basketball and it had been Finney (that's what everyone called him) who had passed Clyde the fatal ball.

Clyde gave Finney a resigned smile. 'Me and Mr Chandra didn't exactly hit it off from the start. I think he's jealous of my popularity.'

Finney rolled his eyes. 'Your trouble is you don't know when to lay off.'

'Yeah. Being funny is a curse. Me and the Wolfman – life's just one big shaggy dog story.'

Finney shook his head. He had to get on; he'd come to pick up supplies from the stationery store for the school art club meeting. Finney was a pretty cool artist. Clyde had seen some of his classwork and stuff from art club, but it was the stuff he didn't show the teachers that impressed Clyde the most – the stuff he couldn't show them. His caricatures. As mostly they were of members of staff and were hilariously funny, Finney tried to keep them under the radar. Clyde reckoned it wouldn't be long before Finney turned out his first Mr Chandra cartoon. The new Head dressed as a one-legged pirate, perhaps: the New Captain on the Bridge! The thought cheered Clyde up – maybe he'd even do one himself; Clyde didn't shout about it, but he was no slouch with a pencil, himself.

The stationery store was right across the corridor from Mr Chandra's office, Finney gave Clyde a grim thumb's down before he went through the door and shut it after him. Clyde got up off the chair he'd been sitting on – this was starting to get beyond a joke: how long was Chandra going to keep him here? Clyde found himself looking at the trophy cabinet. Park Vale wasn't all that good at collecting silverware in the inter-school competitions – the school's football field mauling last night was about par for the course – but there were a few home trophies in there that kids got their names attached to for competitions and achievements at Park Vale. Clyde even had his name on one from this year's sports day. He had come first in the 400 metres. All that running away from assorted alien bad guys turned out to be pretty good training.

He saw his name on the trophy, and couldn't help feeling a small buzz of pride. But then his eye was caught by something else. A reflection behind him. A movement of colour – blue, red and yellow. In the glass of the trophy cupboard he saw a clown slip into the stationery store.

A clown?!

What was going on here?

Clyde spun around. The door to the stationery store was closed. For a moment Clyde wondered if he was seeing things, and then he was crossing the corridor and reaching out for the handle to the stationery store. He felt the hair prickle at the back of his neck. He knew that he hadn't imagined the clown, and just as surely, he knew that meant some kind of trouble.

'Finney?' Clyde said. But there was no answer from inside the stationery store.

Clyde opened the door and stepped inside.

The stationery store was a small room, shelved on every wall, packed with artists' materials. There was no clown in there, and no Finney. But there were papers all over the floor. And outside somewhere Clyde heard a noise – a snigger…

'Finney? Are you messing me around?' Clyde dodged out of the stationery store, willing his friend to be there, a big grin all over his face, winding Clyde up.

But he didn't see Finney. He saw the clown.

He was standing at the other end of the corridor, and Clyde knew there was just no way he could've got there. He hadn't come past Clyde. This was weird.

The clown had orange hair that poked out in spikes either side of his head and on top, other than that he seemed to be bald, with a painted white face and a big red painted mouth. And as clowns went, this one didn't look in the least bit funny.

'Hey!' Clyde yelled and started running towards the clown.

From somewhere it pulled a gigantic multi-coloured handkerchief and gave Clyde a huge grin of yellowing, sharp teeth and a wave. For a moment the clown was completely hidden by the massive handkerchief – and then the handkerchief floated to the ground and the clown had gone.

Clyde pulled up, stunned. The handkerchief lay at his feet and there was no sign of the clown.

Then he heard it snigger again. The noise came from the boys' toilets. The door was right by him. Clyde took a breath and collected his nerve and followed the sound of the clown's laughter – but the toilets were empty.

Clyde quickly kicked open the door to each of the toilet stalls, but the clown wasn't in there.

'He's behind you!'

The voice was sing-song, like someone at a pantomime. Only quiet. And sinister.

Clyde spun around.

There was the clown. In the mirror behind the washbasins.

Clyde's eyes snapped across the room. The clown wasn't there. Only in the mirror. He had a red balloon on a string in his hand.

Clyde gasped. 'Who – what are you?'

The clown looked hurt. Clyde noticed that his

eyes were like small black dots on discs of silver. They weren't human eyes, Clyde thought. Yeah, like appearing in a mirror with no body to give a reflection, didn't give that away! But when the clown spoke it was with a strong American drawl. Like someone from the southern states.

'All I want to do,' said the clown, 'is give you a balloon.'

And as he spoke, the clown's hand passed out of the mirror, the balloon floating on a string.

And the door to the toilets flew open behind him.

'Langer! I've been looking for you!'

Clyde spun around. Mr Chandra stood in the doorway, furious.

'Why aren't you outside my office?'

Clyde kind of thought that was obvious – he'd been chasing a freaky clown that was coming at him out of a mirror – but when he looked back, the only thing he saw in the mirror was his own reflection and that of the steamed-up Head Teacher.

All the same, Clyde's luck had run its course with Mr Chandra. There was no way he couldn't give him some sort of explanation – and, besides, there was Finney to think about.

'Look,' Clyde started, 'I know this is going to sound weird, but I think Dave Finn's been taken.'

'Taken?'

'Abducted. Like those other kids.'

'Langer, if this is some sort of joke.'

'I saw the guy who did it!'

And even as Clyde said it, he knew that this wasn't going to work. He should have thought this through properly. He should have probably kept his mouth shut.

But, to give Mr Chandra his due, he did what he could to check out Clyde's story, whether he believed it or not. Clyde didn't tell him anything about the mirror. He just said he'd chased the clown and lost him, and thought he might have ducked into the toilets to hide. But it wasn't long before the Head's scepticism won out. It didn't take much to confirm that Dave Finn hadn't shown up for class that afternoon, and it hadn't taken much longer for the school's security cameras to show him that there had been no multi-coloured clown on the school premises.

To Mr Chandra, as Clyde sat before him in his office, this was starting to have all the hallmarks of a schoolboy prank.

'It's not a prank, I swear,' Clyde told him.

'So why didn't anyone else see this clown? Why didn't the security cameras pick up a clown? I think it's the sort of thing we would notice, Langer.'

'I don't know, sir. Did the cameras pick up Finney leaving the school?'

The Head didn't answer. They hadn't.

'No,' said Clyde. 'Didn't think so. Just like the other kids. Vanished without a trace. Except this time, I saw something.'

'A clown.'

Clyde really had to bite down hard on the anger he felt rising up. All the same, he felt himself getting up out of the chair and snapping, 'I tell jokes, not lies, sir! I should have known you wouldn't listen.'

It was a good thing there was someone that would.

Only Clyde wasn't going to be able to talk to him until school was over. And that was another three hours. Boy, it was tough work saving the human race on a comprehensive school timetable. And Luke had double physics and chemistry this afternoon so Clyde wasn't even going to be able to tell him what he'd seen until the home bell. By the time it went Clyde was going out of his head with frustration.

He caught up with Luke at the school gates where Luke was chatting to the new girl, Rani. Clyde felt a momentary spike of jealousy – it looked like maybe Luke was getting over Maria pretty fast. But he pushed it aside. There were more important things to deal with.

'Hi, Clyde,' said Rani as he joined them.

'Hi,' said Clyde. 'Look, do you mind, Rani? Me and Luke, we've got some business to discuss.'

Luke's brow furrowed. 'Business?'

'Yeah. Boys Only Business.'

Luke wasn't sure that he really knew what Clyde was talking about, but Rani told them that she'd leave them to it, anyway. Clyde thanked her and reassured her it didn't mean he was giving her the cold shoulder, or anything, and drew Luke across to the opposite side of the road. As they walked he quickly filled Luke in on the clown. And no way was this clown anything you'd find running around a circus ring with a bucket of water.

'You think it's an alien?' Luke asked.

'We know aliens have kidnapped kids before. Remember Kudlak?'

Neither of them was hardly likely to forget General Kudlak who had been using a laser game centre in town to kidnap kids to fight a war on the other side of the cosmos. Luke and Clyde had both wound up on an Uvodni spaceship run by a computer programmed for war and sent crazy by the concept of peace.

'Why would an alien be dressed as a clown?' Luke asked.

It was a fair question, but Clyde had gone through a pretty rough day.

'So you don't believe me, either. Thanks a lot, mate.'

Luke reassured him. 'Of course I believe you. I just don't understand it.'

Clyde managed a smile, 'Well there's a first.'

But the smile didn't last – out of the corner of his eye he caught a flash of moving red, blue and yellow...

'There he is!'

Luke spun around, but saw nothing.

'Come on!'

Clyde was already running. Luke took off after him.

With Clyde just ahead, the two of them hurtled across the streets, dodged down side roads and cut across verges. Luke never saw anything, but Clyde kept catching glimpses of the clown. One moment he would be walking casually across a road, mindless of approaching traffic, the next he would be leaning nonchalantly against a wall. But whenever Clyde looked again, the clown would be gone. It was like chasing smoke.

Then Clyde caught sight of him in an alleyway behind a block of garages.

'There he is!' he cried at Luke.

But by the time he looked back the clown had gone again. All that remained was a red balloon floating on a string tied to a drainpipe.

Clyde looked about him as he approached the balloon. There was no point in running any more. There was no clue as to which way the clown might have gone. And the balloon suggested that the clown had decided the game was over.

'What happened to him?' Luke asked.

'Search me,' Clyde said. 'But he left this behind.'

And Clyde reached out for the balloon.

A girl cried out, 'Don't touch it!'

Both boys spun around to see Rani at the end of the alleyway; she had clearly been running after them.

'I don't know why,' she yelled, running towards them. 'Just don't!'

As she reached Clyde and Luke they turned

back towards the balloon.

BANG!

It burst.

Chapter Five

The revelations of Rani

'I've been seeing it for days. It just keeps showing up. Always on the other side of the street. Or, like today, at the window in class. Not close-up. A clown dressed in red, blue and yellow.'

They were close to Bannerman Road now. Rani walked with Luke on one said and Clyde on the other. She had told them everything about the clown that had been haunting her and now seemed to have latched on to Clyde.

'But you haven't told anyone about it?' asked

Luke. 'I mean, if you've been seeing it all over the place for a week now...'

Rani couldn't believe what she was hearing. 'What am I going to say, listen mum and dad, I don't want to worry you, but I'm seeing clowns that no one else can see?'

He shrugged, 'Why not?'

'You want them to get me locked up?'

'Why would they do that?'

Rani turned from Luke to Clyde, wide-eyed with disbelief. 'What planet is he from?'

Clyde grinned, he'd been enjoying Luke digging himself a hole with Rani. 'Oh, Earth. Mostly.'

But Rani wasn't that impressed with Clyde, either.

'You're so funny, Clyde. No wonder the Head Teacher loves you so much.'

Something struck Luke about the way she had said it. Like her tongue had tripped her when she mentioned the new Head. Like she had been about to say something else.

'Rani,' Clyde said, 'whoever this clown is, we're going to have to leave it to the cops.'

They were in Bannerman Road now, right outside Maria's old house, and he was thinking about what Sarah Jane had said that morning, and he knew she had been right. If this clown was an alien they were going to have to deal with it without Rani finding out. He caught Luke's eye, and he backed Clyde up.

'Clyde's right. This is nothing to do with us.'

But Rani was having a difficult time controlling her anger. 'Look, there's something happening here that doesn't make everyday sense! Maybe you can ignore it because it doesn't go with your MP3 player and your designer trainers, but I can't! I've got to know what's going on!'

Clyde glanced at Luke and said quietly, 'Oh, Sarah Jane is going to love this one.'

A car drawing up outside her house had caught Rani's attention. Quickly she looked back at the boys, looking grave. 'There's something I've got to tell you. Something you ought to know.'

'You're from another planet,' said Clyde. 'I already guessed.' The way things went around here, it certainly wouldn't have surprised him.

At his shoulder, Luke said, 'Actually, Clyde, it's worse than that.'

Luke had seen the car pull up, as well. He had seen who was getting out of it. And now Clyde did, too.

Clyde's world went into free fall. 'Oh, no. Rani,

tell me there's a good reason why our new Head just pulled up outside your house that doesn't include the word dad.'

As Mr Chandra got out of the car and walked towards them Rani tried to quickly explain. 'Honestly, he's all right, really. It's just his job.'

But Clyde was unimpressed – that was what they had said about Doctor Frankenstein!

As Mr Chandra joined the kids, casting a suspicious look at Clyde, the front door of Maria's old house opened. Rani's mum came out and headed towards them, all smiles.

'Haresh!' she cried at Mr Chandra. 'Don't worry, there are still plenty of boxes for you to open. Rani, my darling, how was your first day at school?' And she smothered Rani in a big hug. 'Did your dad go all Captain Bligh again?'

Haresh Chandra caught the smile between Luke and Clyde and simmered, 'I do not go all Captain Bligh.'

But Rani told her mum that he did, just a bit. And introduced Luke and Clyde.

'Luke Smith,' Luke told Gita, offering her his hand. 'Pleased to meet you.'

The name set off a firework inside Haresh's head. 'Luke Smith?'

He turned towards Luke, his eyes alight with interest.

'He's my son. I'm Sarah Jane Smith.'

Luke saw that his mum had crossed the road to them. Haresh reached out and shook her hand, a smile spreading across his face. It was the sort of thing Clyde had never expected to see. He thought Mr Chandra had the kind of face that only cracked to bark and order.

'I've been looking at Luke's results for the last year. Very, very impressive.'

Sarah Jane slipped an arm around Luke's shoulders; it was part pride and part protection.

'He's very gifted,' she said simply.

The trouble with Luke's intelligence was that it made him stand out. He couldn't help it. And the last thing that Sarah Jane needed was for that to attract too much attention. Some questions about Luke would be difficult to answer.

'Sarah's a journalist,' Gita told Rani.

Rani's face lit up with excitement. 'For real? That's fantastic! I'm really interested in being a reporter when I leave school, Sarah Jane. Maybe I can come over some time?'

Sarah Jane smiled tightly. If there was any chance at all that Rani Chandra had the makings of

The sinister alien clown, Odd Bob.
He feeds on fear to survive.

Odd Bob stalks Tony Warner, just before Tony mysteriously disappears.

Clyde and Luke meet Rani, who has just moved into Bannerman Road.

Haresh Chandra, the new Head Teacher at Park Vale School.

Sarah Jane and Clyde enter Spellman's Magical Museum of the Circus.

"Elijah Spellman, at your service. Madame," said the ringmaster.

The mysterious Spellman senses Sarah Jane's fear of clowns.

Clyde is amazed that the story of the Pied Piper of Hamelin, is true.

Rani screams as one of the mannequin clowns comes to life and grabs her arm.

Sarah Jane uses her sonic lipstick to try and stop the approaching clowns.

Mr Spellman is controlling the
mannequin clowns by telekinesis.

The day of the clown. The scary mannequins advance on Sarah Jane and her friends.

Rani and Clyde try to stop the children, who are being controlled by Spellman, from going to his museum.

a journalist – and from what Gita had said earlier, she did – then the last place Sarah Jane wanted her was on her side of Bannerman Road.

'Well,' she said bluntly, 'I am rather busy.'

Then Sarah Jane hated herself a little when she saw the disappointment in Rani's eyes.

Clyde, meanwhile, was feeling robbed of the spotlight.

'And I'm Clyde Langer,' he told Gita. 'The joker in the pack. Apparently.'

Clyde enjoyed Mr Chandra's discomfort.

'Oh, and I see clowns that don't exist.'

Haresh Chandra gave Clyde a look that fried and announced that he was hungry and that, if Sarah Jane would excuse them, his family had a busy evening ahead of them.

Sarah Jane understood, of course, and wished them well in Bannerman Road. Then, as the Chandras headed inside their new home, Sarah Jane crossed back to her big house on the other side of the road with Luke and Clyde. As they went, Rani looked back and saw that all three were instantly wrapped up in some intense conversation.

'Rani!' Gita was calling. 'Come and see your new room!'

Rani smiled, for the moment any worries about strange clowns pushed aside by the thrill of the move into a new home.

The Chandras were from Nottingham originally. Both her father's and mother's parents had settled there back in the sixties when they moved to England from India. Rani had always thought how brave they had been. England must have seemed so strange and she knew that not everyone had welcomed them. But the Chandras and her mother's family, the Vermas, had settled well in Nottingham and had flourished. Their families had since spread across the country. Rani had lived in London since she was ten. They had moved down there when Haresh got a job as the head of the history department at a school in Camden. The opportunity to take over the vacancy left by Mr Blakeman's sudden disappearance at Park Vale had been too good for Haresh to pass on. And so they had moved to Bannerman Road.

Now Rani stood in her new bedroom that was filled with unopened boxes, and tried to imagine what her life was going to be like here.

Downstairs she heard her mum call up, 'Coffee!'

Rani made her way down to the kitchen and found her mum and dad discussing Dave Finn's disappearance. Haresh might not have been convinced by Clyde's story, but he had cared enough to look hard and make some phone calls – all of which had confirmed that Finney was nowhere to be found. Maybe a clown hadn't taken him, but he had vanished without trace.

Haresh had brought a plastic bag in with him from the car. Inside it he had Finney's schoolbooks.

'The police want to look at them,' he explained. 'There's a chance that something was worrying the boy and he's run away. Kids sometimes write things down. There might be some sort of a clue here.'

Rani glanced across at the books over the top of her coffee cup and wondered, if there was a clue in them would the police even be able to recognise it? The police were the last people likely to understand just how weird things were around here.

Gita shuddered as she thought about the disappearances. She pushed her worries aside with the more immediate concern for where they were going to sleep that night. The removal men hadn't listened to a word she had said about where she wanted the bed. They had put it up against the bathroom wall, and there was no way she was sleeping like that tonight – it was such bad Feng Shui! She harried her husband out of the kitchen and up the stairs to fix things.

And as the door closed behind them, Rani fell on Dave Finn's books.

If there was a clue in them she knew that she would spot it. Because Rani knew what she was looking for.

She found the first drawing of the clown at the back of his English Lit book. Finney's drawing was good. In a nightmarish way. Rani recognised the clown straight away.

There were other pictures. She found them as she hurriedly flicked through Finney's other books. Each one sketched with intensity, each one more frightening than the last. The clown with the balloon. The clown smiling with rotting teeth. The clown reaching towards her. There was no question; the same thing that had haunted Dave Finn was stalking her. And that could only mean one thing.

She pushed herself back from the kitchen table where she had the books spread out before her. And she saw the clown staring in at her from the window.

Its grease-paint face was pressed up against the glass, its red nose squashed. Its strange silver eyes danced with a malevolent delight.

'No,' Rani gasped. 'You're not there!'

She closed her eyes tight, willing the thing away, knowing that when she opened them again it would be gone – just as it always was, like the memory of a nightmare.

But the clown hadn't gone. It was in the kitchen now. It was right by the table leaning towards her, grinning, holding out a red balloon.

Rani tried to cry out, but all that escaped was a breath that felt for the world like her last.

Then the kitchen door flew open behind her.

It was Gita. 'Rani, you've got a visitor!'

Rani swung around to see her mum with Luke.

The clown had vanished.

She looked back at Luke; she thought that she had never been so happy to see anyone in her whole life.

Chapter Six

Spellman's magical museum

'Of course Mr Chandra was never going to believe you, Clyde. Nor would the police,' said Sarah Jane.

Clyde had started filling her in on the day's events the moment they started to cross Bannerman Road, and as soon as Rani was out of earshot. Sarah Jane had led them straight to the attic.

The attic in Clyde's house was little more than a dusty cupboard packed with junk; Sarah Jane's attic was something all together different. This was where she worked and there was a desk with a computer at which she wrote her newspaper stories; this was also the place in which she sometimes saved the world, and built into the wall was another kind of computer entirely.

'Children don't vanish out of closed rooms. It's impossible,' she said. 'As far as people like the police and Mr Chandra are concerned.'

Unlike the police or Mr Chandra, Sarah Jane believed Clyde's story immediately. She had, after all, seen many things that few others would have believed.

Yet there were still things that Clyde didn't understand about what he had seen. 'If it's an alien that's taking these kids, a clown disguise isn't exactly low profile, is it?'

'But it might know that kids are supposed to like clowns,' suggested Luke.

Sarah Jane shivered. She felt old memories surfacing. Memories that she didn't need.

'Personally, clowns always gave me nightmares,' she said.

'Coulrophobia,' Luke chipped in. 'It's the fear of clowns. Johnny Depp has it.'

Clyde was used to being gob-smacked by Luke's knowledge, but sometimes...

'What encyclopaedia did you find that in?' he

asked, looking at Luke in amazement.

Luke beamed. '*Heat*.'

Clyde rolled his eyes. Sarah Jane was already planning what they had to do next. Obviously Dave Finn's parents were going to be too busy with the police right now to talk to them. Maybe one of Finney's friends would be a good place to start piecing things together.

It was a Monday. That meant training for the school football team, Clyde told her. Finney's best mate was a kid called Steve Wallace who had scored Park Vale's only goal during last week's exit match from the school championships.

Sarah Jane grabbed her coat, eager to collar Steve Wallace before the end of football practice.

'What about Rani?' asked Luke.

'I don't want her involved,' said Sarah Jane.

'But she is involved already,' Luke pointed out. 'And she's determined to find out what's going on. She might be in danger.'

Sarah Jane considered. 'You're right. Someone should keep an eye on her.'

Sounded like a job for Clyde Langer.

Only Luke had some bad news for him. 'I don't think her dad would let you anywhere near her.'

Clyde knew Luke was right, but did he have to

smile quite so much when he told him?

So while Luke was looking after the new girl over the road, Clyde and Sarah Jane were talking to Steve Wallace on the touchline as the rest of the team went through their paces in training for a better challenge season next year. Not that Steve was all that keen on talking. He knew Dave had gone missing, of course, and he would do anything he could to help find him, only when Clyde introduced the woman that was with him he said she was a journalist.

'My dad says journalists are scum. They're like crows picking at road-kill.'

Clyde had met Steve's dad and he wasn't impressed. He made his own walk-out dad look like 'Father of the Year'.

'I suppose he only buys a newspaper to look at the pictures, then?' Clyde taunted. 'Come on, Steve, Sarah Jane is trying to help find Finney.'

Steve shrugged and bounced the football he was holding, 'I don't know anything.'

'Had he been acting strangely?' Sarah Jane asked.

'Not that I saw.'

'What about clowns?' Clyde asked. 'Did he ever say anything about clowns.'

Steve frowned, like why would he?

And then he remembered something.

'There was a clown down by the station. There was me, Finney and Tony Warner. He was handing out tickets.'

Sarah Jane was electrified. 'Tony Warner? The other boy that went missing?'

Steve nodded. 'Him and Finney used to hang around a lot. Anyway they both took a ticket off the clown. I told the weirdo to take a hike.'

As Steve spoke something went off at the back of Clyde's head. He started digging into his pockets. 'Hang on, I'd forgotten all about this. My mum said she'd picked it up at the shops.'

And then he had it, a carelessly folded piece of paper. A ticket.

'That's it,' said Steve. 'One just like that!'

Sarah Jane took the ticket and looked at it. It was designed to look as if the reader were looking through the folded back tent flaps of a big top. A tent decorated with red, yellow and blue stripes. Sarah Jane read the words that floated within the big top...

SPELLMAN'S MAGICAL MUSEUM OF THE CIRCUS.

And at almost the same time, back in Bannerman

Road, Rani and Luke came across exactly the same ticket pinned between the pages of one of Dave Finn's books.

When Luke had shown up in the kitchen earlier he had said he'd come around to help Rani unpack. She thanked him and told him she could really do with the help and had taken him straight up to her room, along with Dave Finn's books. Barely stopping for breath she told him about the clown in the kitchen just moments before he got there, and showed him Finney's pictures.

'This isn't natural, Luke. None of it is! Whatever's going on here – whatever this clown is – it's supernatural.'

Luke looked up from Finney's books, 'I doubt that it's supernatural.'

Rani felt like kicking him – how could he deny what was so obvious? She knew he was clever, but even Luke was never going to come up with a rational explanation for what was happening to her.

'You've got such a closed mind!' she said. 'The supernatural is only science we don't know yet – like life on other planets.'

'No,' he said. 'That's different.'

Aliens existed; ghosts and things that were a part of the supernatural did not. But he wasn't going to tell her any of that. It wasn't really going to help.

'Look, I've got to do something, Luke. Look at Finney's pictures. He was seeing the clown same as I am. That means it's coming after me, like it did him.'

And that was when Luke turned a page and found the ticket. Rani recognised it immediately. She found another just like it among her stuff.

SPELLMAN'S MAGICAL MUSEUM OF THE CIRCUS.

Luke bit his lip, whatever Sarah Jane had said, there was no doubt now that Rani was in real danger.

'You should talk to my mum,' he said. 'Mum understands things like this.'

Rani was already grabbing her coat.

'Where are you going?' he asked.

'Luke, no one understands things like this. But this ticket has got to be some sort of a clue. Are you coming?'

Luke knew there was no way he was going to stop Rani; her eyes were alight with excitement. He had seen the same look in someone else's eyes. And once that happened he knew there was no way you could stop them.

He had seen that same look in Sarah

Jane's eyes.

Only right now there was a quite different look in the eyes of Sarah Jane Smith.

She stood with Clyde just outside Spellman's Magical Museum of the Circus. Its front had been painted to resemble a circus tent and on either side of the door stood life-size clown paintings. To Sarah Jane their wide painted smiles looked more like snarls.

She really, really hated clowns.

'Welcome to the Circus of Horrors,' Clyde said beside her.

Sarah Jane glanced at him. 'You know, Clyde, occasionally your sense of humour really leaves something to be desired.'

'Who said I was joking?' he asked.

Sarah Jane shuddered and forced herself to lead Clyde over the threshold and into the museum.

Inside they found themselves in a strange, dimly lit world where circus music played softly in the background, accompanied occasionally by the roar and gasp of a recorded crowd. There were posters on the walls advertising the great world-famous circuses of the past, and pictures of circus acts that seemed to go back decades. Clyde took it all in with mystified wonder. He stopped to pat the trunk of a stuffed elephant head and rolled his eyes.

'Like museums don't normally creep me out – all those stuffed animals, old bones and mummies – but this place doesn't just take the biscuit, man, this place gets the whole Christmas tin.'

And behind them a mechanical clown in a glass case started to laugh hysterically.

Sarah Jane nearly jumped out of her skin.

That was when a spotlight suddenly illuminated the tall man standing in the corner. He was dressed like a ringmaster, complete with top hat, whip and waxed moustache. For a moment she thought he was a waxwork, then he bowed...

'Welcome! Welcome, to Spellman's Magical Museum of the Circus, and the story of the most wondrous family entertainment in the world.'

He spoke with a German accent, 'From the tumblers and jugglers of ancient Rome, to the father of the modern circus, a sergeant major in the 15th Light Dragoons!'

'Mr Spellman, I presume?'

Spellman bowed, tipping his top hat, 'Elijah Spellman, at your service, Madame.'

Creepy, thought Clyde. But what else had

he expected?

'My name is Sarah Jane Smith. I'm a journalist. This is my friend, Clyde. We're here to talk to you about clowns.'

Spellman's eyes lit up, 'Ah! The Princes of the Sawdust Ring. This way, please.'

He led them along a corridor and into another room and Sarah Jane felt the blood turn to ice in her veins. The room was filled with life-size clown mannequins. Pale-faced clowns, tramp clowns, bald clowns, crazy-haired clowns. Every clown you could think of. And every one of them seemed to be watching Sarah Jane, every one of them silently taunting her and laughing at her fear of them.

She felt her pulse racing and told herself to get a grip – what had happened to her had been a long, long time ago. And it had been nothing, really. Nothing, she told herself, just a trick of the light.

'Mankind has always needed someone to make them laugh, slave or king,' Elijah Spellman was saying, as he walked around the room, in between the mannequins.

'Maybe you can drop a note to my new Head,' Clyde suggested, wryly.

Spellman continued, ignoring Clyde, 'The Pharaohs had fools, so did Native Americans. We had the harlequin and, in the Middle Ages, the jester.'

But Sarah Jane had had enough of his shtick, 'Mr Spellman, it's not so much the clown's showbiz history I'm interested in as their reputation for scaring people.'

Spellman looked at her, and Sarah Jane realised uncomfortably that the ringmaster saw her own uneasiness among the clowns. He smiled, 'Ah, the fear of the painted smile.'

'They used to paint clowns on the walls of children's wards, but when they were asked every child said the pictures scared them. Children sense things,' said Sarah Jane. 'I know.'

From behind her, Clyde called out. He had found something. Sarah Jane turned around and saw a reproduction of an old picture, a man with some sort of pipe, dressed in red, yellow and blue.

'Those are the colours of the clown I saw,' Clyde said.

But Sarah Jane had seen this picture before, and this wasn't a clown.

'This is the Pied Piper,' she said. 'He wasn't a clown. He rid Hamelin of a plague of rats by playing a magical tune on his flute, then when the town refused to pay him he went back and took all their children.'

Spellman spoke close to Sarah Jane's ear, 'The oldest and most accurate picture of the Pied Piper. The colours of his costume signify he was a travelling entertainer and, I'm afraid, even clowns have their dark days.'

'And that's exactly the sort of clown I'm interested in. One that makes children disappear,' said Sarah Jane.

But Clyde was confused. 'The Pied Piper was a fairytale. Wasn't it?'

'Myths, legends, fairy tales – every story has its inspiration, Clyde.' Then Sarah Jane turned back to Spellman – but he was no longer there.

'Mr Spellman?'

'Where did he go?'

'I don't know,' Sarah Jane said. She was starting to feel nervous, and she didn't think it had anything to do with any clown phobia – this was a feeling in her gut that she had felt countless times before, and it had saved her life just as often. 'I think we should get out of here. Now.'

They turned to go – and found Luke and Rani standing there.

'Luke!'

But Luke was just as shocked. 'Mum!'

'What are you doing here?' Clyde demanded.

But Rani wanted answers, too. 'What are we doing here? What are you doing here?'

Luke was telling Sarah Jane that she had told him to stay with Rani – so he'd had to come with her when she set out for this place.

And Rani heard that and her confusion went critical. 'Am I missing something?'

Clyde told Luke he had been supposed to keep Rani out of the action.

And she wanted to know, 'What action?'

She got her answer when one of the clown mannequins grabbed her hand.

Rani screamed with shock and Clyde tore the mannequin's hand from her. Around them the mannequins were starting to move, coming to life.

Rani took it all in, unable to believe her eyes. 'What's happening? They're alive!'

'Run!' Sarah Jane shouted.

Together they burst out of the clown room and into the passageway – and the clown mannequins followed. They didn't move quickly, and their movements were staccato, like clockwork toys. Sarah Jane had no doubt they were no less dangerous, for all that.

'What happened to Spellman,' Clyde demanded.

'He's controlling them,' Sarah Jane told him, keeping her eyes peeled for more clowns. 'I think they're like puppets – probably under some sort of telekinetic control.'

'Walking puppets? Telekinetic control?' Rani was having a hard time keeping up.

'He's controlling them with his mind,' Luke told her helpfully.

'I know what it means, Luke. Who is Spellman?'

'Probably an alien,' he told her.

'You know, that sounded just like you said 'alien'.'

More mannequin clowns appeared ahead of them, blocking off their escape, reaching out for them.

Rani saw Sarah Jane pull something from her bag and cry out to them, 'Stand back!'

There was some sort of electronic buzz and suddenly the clowns were frozen.

Rani's mind was falling over itself, 'What was that?'

'Sonic lipstick,' Sarah Jane said, twisting the top back on something that looked – well, like a lipstick. 'Never leave home without it!'

She told them it would hold the clowns for a while, but they had to get out of there quickly, and she set off, leading the way.

'Aliens,' Rani called after Sarah Jane. 'Luke said aliens!'

'Actually,' Clyde corrected, 'he just said alien.'

'And it will be still around here somewhere,' warned Sarah Jane. 'Come on. There's no time for explanations.'

Clyde took Rani's hand, 'She's right. And from what I've seen, one alien can be as much trouble as a whole invasion.'

Rani gave up. None of this made sense. None of it. But she didn't have to understand it to see that they were right, they had to get out of there. Whatever was going on here, it wasn't good.

They hit the front doors at a run. But they didn't give. Rani saw Sarah Jane pull out her lipstick thing again, but this time it just buzzed and the doors stayed shut.

'He's sealed the doors,' she said.

'Telekinesis,' Luke offered quickly. 'The same way he animated the mannequins.'

Sarah Jane was grim. 'Whatever we're dealing with here, it's extremely powerful.'

'And it's got us trapped,' gasped Rani.

Sarah Jane turned on her and spoke firmly. 'No. It just thinks it has.'

Spellman appeared from nowhere. 'Oh, no, Miss Smith. I am convinced of it.'

Rani took in Spellman in his ringmaster gear. 'Are you really an alien?'

Sarah Jane put herself between Spellman and Rani. 'Stay back, Rani. Leave this to me.'

'I just never thought an alien would dress like such a geek,' she said.

Sarah Jane stood defiantly before Spellman, 'Who are you? And what do you want?'

Spellman looked at her, a smile creeping across his face. 'Who am I?'

And Spellman began to blur, the red and white of his ringmaster's outfit shifting colours, his face changing, his clothes altering. Spellman had gone, and Sarah Jane was facing the man in the ancient picture, the man that had charmed away Hamelin's rats, and then its children.

'I am the Pied Piper,' he said. 'Who conjured away a whole town's infants, and has chilled the hearts of parents for more than seven centuries.'

His outline blurred again, his shape changing before their eyes. And Rani gasped with horror as she recognised what now stood before them, a red balloon in his hand.

'And now I am Odd Bob the Clown,' he said in that Southern States drawl, 'who snatches children in the heartbeat that their mother's back is turned. I am the thing that lives in the darkest corner.'

Sarah Jane pressed back against the others, protectively, her mind scrambling hopelessly for something she could do to defend them from this thing, as Odd Bob took a step towards them, and another...

'I am all these things and more. I am all that you fear the most.'

He came closer, and began to slowly reach out towards them, grinning, teasing, terrifying...

'And you are mine to feed on! Fear me! You are mine!'

Chapter Seven

Rani's choice

'**D**on't let him touch you!' Sarah Jane screamed, as she lunged past Odd Bob, grabbed a fire extinguisher from the wall and fired the freezing gas at the clown-thing.

The carbon dioxide clouded around Odd Bob, but that horrible rotted-toothed smile never faltered, in fact it grew.

'Oh, sweet, sweet fear,' he purred.

Clyde could see this wasn't going their way at all. He hit the sealed museum door with his shoulder as hard as he could. It didn't shift a bit. It didn't even give in the door hinges the way it might had someone turned the lock. Odd Bob or Spellman,

8 F T Y 3 B N A 1 K L D 6 R E 9 S X 5 P O C Z **67**

the Pied Piper, or whoever had them captive here, had jammed it solid with his telekinesis. All the same Clyde wasn't about to give in, so he rammed it with his shoulder again. Just as hard.

Nothing.

He flashed a look at Luke. 'Give me a hand!'

And together the boys shoved at the door, as Odd Bob reached out for Rani.

Quickly, she shrank back. 'Why are you coming after me? I don't even know what you are!'

'But you have a ticket,' he said, almost gently. 'You're mine.'

'Get away from her!' Sarah Jane shouted, and used the butt end of the dead extinguisher to keep him away – but Odd Bob tore the empty can from her hands and threw it across the lobby.

Odd Bob snarled at Sarah Jane. His painted lips curled back, and he snarled like a rabid wolf.

Sarah Jane stood her ground, 'I'm not scared of you!'

Odd Bob smiled again, and Sarah Jane wasn't sure which was worse. 'But you are scared of me, Sarah Jane Smith. I can taste it!'

Sarah Jane shook her head – tried to tell him that he was wrong – but it was no good, the words wouldn't come. Her mouth was too dry to speak.

And Odd Bob took another step towards her...

'Of all the things you've seen, Sarah Jane, of all the things out of the dark that you have fought, it's me that lives in your nightmares. The painted face of a clown.'

Luke lunged his shoulder at the immoveable door and threw a desperate glance towards Sarah Jane. He saw her, paralysed with fear as the clown reached out for her.

'Mum!' he yelled.

Rani's phone went off. It was the sound of a baby singing some pop song that he thought might have been Kylie. It was dreadful – and it stopped Odd Bob in his tracks.

At the same instant the museum door flew open against Clyde's shoulder.

'Quick!' he shouted. 'We're out!'

Sarah Jane took one glance back at Odd Bob and saw that the clown seemed to be frozen.

'Run!' she yelled, and followed the three kids out of the door towards her car.

Rani pulled the phone from her pocket as she ran towards the little car. 'It's my Mum!'

'Don't answer it!' Luke told her.

'What?'

'You can't tell her what just happened!'

'I don't know what happened!' she said, looking back at the museum, and silencing the phone.

There was no sign of Odd Bob following, but Sarah Jane thought it wouldn't be long before he came after them.

'The phone's electromagnetic wave must have temporarily interfered with Spellman's energies. They must have a similar frequency. Quickly, in the car!'

Sarah Jane had the car open, Luke and Clyde piled in, but Rani hesitated. 'Isn't someone going to tell me what's going on?'

Sarah Jane glared at her across the car's roof. 'Rani, there's a time and a place for an interview. And being chased by a clown from outer space is most definitely not it!'

Sarah Jane jumped behind the wheel, Rani took one last confused look back at the museum and got into the car, her head whirling with questions – but Sarah Jane wouldn't say anything until a few minutes later when they were back in Bannerman Road. Which was when her mum rang the mobile again. The baby-voice version of the Kylie song set Clyde's teeth on edge.

'Okay, annoying ring tones have their uses – I think we've all learned that today. But they are still annoying,' he complained.

'It's my mum,' Rani said as they got out of the car on Sarah Jane's drive. 'What do I tell her?'

'You're on your way home,' Sarah Jane told her.

Rani couldn't believe she was hearing it. 'Just like that? You expect me to go home?'

Sarah Jane was heading for her front door, as if the subject was closed.

But Luke was on Rani's side. 'Mum, I think you have to tell her everything.'

Sarah Jane spun around, staring. 'No, I told you. Both of you...'

Clyde winced as the phone continued to wail the baby-song. 'Please, Sarah Jane. That phone is doing my head in!'

Sarah Jane took Rani's phone and turned it off, then she stood for a moment without saying anything, just looking into Rani's eyes, as if she were trying to see something beyond them.

'I'm going to offer you a choice,' she said eventually. 'Cross over the road, go back to your parents and the life you had before you moved here. And nothing will have changed.'

Rani glanced from Sarah Jane to Luke and Clyde who stood a little way off, watching. She tried to read their faces, to understand what she was on the edge of here...

'Or you can come with me,' said Sarah Jane. 'If you do that, nothing will ever be the same again.'

Chapter Eight

The attic

There was never really any question, and of course Sarah Jane had known as much, Rani was never going to go back across the road and forget about what she had seen that day. Some people would. Some people would lie to themselves and deny the evidence of their own eyes to preserve their narrow-minded view of reality. But Sarah Jane had known that Rani wasn't like that. When she had looked into her eyes on the driveway she had seen something that she knew well – a look in the tall girl's eyes that Sarah Jane saw every time she caught her own reflection in a mirror.

And now she led Rani into the attic, and watched with a delight that she tried to hide as the new girl from across the road took in the room with eyes like saucers.

'How cool is this? This is where you work?' she asked, her eyes skimming around the attic – from Sarah Jane's cluttered workstation to the old dentists' chair by the attic window and the telescope that stood with it – from the bookshelves that held everything from scientific manuals to old tomes on myths and legends, to the old long cased clock by the door – from the heavyweight safe in the wall to a collection of strangely shaped metallic objects that Rani couldn't even begin to guess at their identity.

She picked up one of the objects, 'What's this?'

Quickly but gently, Sarah Jane took it from her. 'That's a distress beacon from a Cylethian scoutship. If you're not careful with it you could have an inter-galactic rescue team landing on the corner of Bannerman Road. You might be a hundred and fourteen by the time they got here – Cylith is a very long way off – but they would come.'

'Aliens?' Rani asked, shaking her head. 'More aliens? Okay, any second now and my alarm is going to go off and it's my second day at Park Vale. A new school with your dad as the Head – any one would have nutty dreams.'

Over Sarah Jane's shoulder she could see Clyde and Luke smiling. For an instant Rani thought maybe this was all some really big joke they were playing on her. But how could it be? That clown thing had been following her for days. She didn't know how any of it could be real – but it was.

'All right, Rani, this is what we do,' said Sarah Jane, fixing her with serious gaze. 'When aliens come to Earth – and they do, all the time – if they are friendly and they need help, we're here to give it.'

Clyde sat down on the steps of the attic where it split into two levels. 'On the other hand, if they're looking for trouble, we give 'em that, too.'

Sarah Jane flashed him a scolding look. 'I wouldn't have put it quite like that.'

'But we have saved the world twelve times,' said Luke.

Rani gaped, 'For real?'

Sarah Jane shrugged. 'No one is keeping score.'

'Except for Luke,' said Clyde.

Luke flashed Clyde a look and Clyde beamed back one of his big grins.

'What's important are the rules,' Sarah Jane said. 'We look after each other. We respect all life – whatever planet it is from – and we tell no one what we do. Do you understand, Rani? No one.'

'Yeah. I understand.'

Oh, yeah. She really understood all of this. This morning all she had to worry about was a new school and the possibility that she might have been going mad. Now she was in the middle of some weird Ealing version of *Men in Black*!

Sarah Jane turned from Rani, 'Mr Smith, I need you.'

Rani caught the movement in the brickwork out of the corner of her eye. As she spun towards it she could hear hydraulic engines somewhere behind the wall thundering into life.

Oh, no! This just could not get any weirder!

Clouds of gas escaped from the void that opened in the brickwork.

'What's happening?'

Clyde had got up from the step and now stood beside her, 'Don't worry, it's only Mr Smith.'

And Mr Smith slid into view.

'Yes, Sarah Jane, how can I help you?' Mr Smith asked.

'It's a computer!' Rani gasped. 'A talking computer! You've got a talking computer in your wall!'

'Actually he's a Xylok,' Clyde corrected Rani. 'A crystalline life form. Just about the smartest in the galaxy. But computer is close enough.

A supercomputer.'

Luke looked at Rani and smiled. 'Do you know your mouth is open?'

Rani shut it quickly, but still gazed in wonder as Sarah Jane approached Mr Smith.

'I need you to tell me everything you know about the Pied Piper, and a clown called Odd Bob.'

'Ah,' said Mr Smith, 'this has to do with the children that have gone missing.'

'Yeah. Pied Piper kind of gives it away, Mr Smith,' taunted Clyde.

'He's an alien supercomputer, and you cheek him?' Rani asked, a part of her still trying to tell herself that this was just some crazy dream.

Probably something Dad cooked up.

It made more sense than any of this being real.

'Me and Mr Smith have got a sort of special relationship,' Clyde was telling her proudly. 'Since he kidnapped me and tried to destroy the planet. Oh, but everything is cool now.'

And Rani's mind did cartwheels.

But Mr Smith was speaking again. 'Actually, the name Odd Bob is equally significant. Across America in the period 1932 to 1940 there was a spate of disappearances of children all connected to a travelling clown known as Odd Bob.'

As Mr Smith spoke his big screen carried images of old American newspaper cuttings. Photograph after photograph of children that went missing and were never found.

Sarah Jane absorbed this information solemnly, 'So many...'

'What about the Pied Piper?' Rani asked without thinking.

'I'm sorry, I don't think we've been introduced,' said Mr Smith.

'This is Rani,' Sarah Jane explained. 'She's... just visiting. What about the Pied Piper?'

Mr Smith's screen began to carry images of the fairytale character, among them the one that was hanging in Spellman's museum.

'A legendary figure that in 1284 rid the German town of Hamelin of a plague of rats by means of a magical tune. When the town refused to pay his fee he enchanted away all its children.

'The story has become known as a fairytale, but it is a matter of historical fact that Hamelin lost its children.'

'Whoa!' Rani exploded. 'You mean it's true?'

'Fairy stories and legends often have some basis in fact,' Clyde told Rani, trying to look learned.

Sarah Jane caught his eye and smiled, then dug out Clyde's ticket to the circus museum and placed it on the computer's analysis tray and asked Mr Smith if he could identify any alien energy.

'There is an energy trace, but I am unable to identify with no comparable data for analysis.'

Clyde whistled, that meant this was something from way off, he told Rani.

But Sarah Jane wasn't done yet. She asked Mr Smith to show her the historical extra-terrestrial records for Lower Saxony in the Thirteenth Century. Instantly the computer's big screen was filled with an ancient map of Germany that showed Hamelin. Over it were superimposed graphics that indicated meteor impacts and known alien landings of the period.

Luke spotted something: there had been an impact in the Weserbergland Mountains, not far from Hamelin.

Mr Smith told them that a meteor fragment had landed there in 1283.

Rani felt a thrill of excitement. 'The year before the Piper appeared! Yes! The Piper was in the meteor! Result!'

But Mr Smith came back, like a teacher unimpressed by an answer in class. 'The meteor had a circumference of thirty point two centimetres. An unlikely spacecraft, Rani.'

Rani felt crushed, but Sarah Jane couldn't help but admire her enthusiasm, and flashed a warm smile.

'All the same,' Sarah Jane said to Mr Smith, 'what do we know about it?'

'The meteorite is currently on loan to the UK.'

Clyde gasped, 'You mean it's here?'

'He came with it,' said Luke.

'Perhaps,' continued Mr Smith, 'if I were able to analyse a fragment, I could provide more information on the energy sample.'

Sarah Jane asked Mr Smith for the meteorite's whereabouts.

'The Pharos Institute,' he said.

Sarah Jane raised an eyebrow and exchanged a look with Clyde and Luke.

Rani caught the look. 'What's wrong?'

The Pharos Institute was a scientific foundation that had been established over twenty years ago and worked in fields generally known as para-science – science that most men and women in white coats considered quackery. Ghosts, telepathy, precognition, clairvoyance – these were some of the areas in which Pharos scientists conducted their experiments. Sarah Jane didn't believe in ghosts, but she applauded the Pharos scientists' open-minded approach to establishing whether or not they existed. Some months ago they had been conducting experiments in the mind's ability to move objects by thought. They had nearly ended with the moon crashing into Earth – thanks to the Slitheen and Mr Smith. And Luke.

But the director of the institute, Professor Celeste Rivers, had been grateful for Sarah Jane's intervention and her help in keeping its role in events quiet. Sarah Jane was pretty sure that Professor Rivers would remember that she owed her a favour.

Yet there was little that they could do now, and Sarah Jane told Rani that she would walk her home.

It was dark now, and the stars had come out in a clear, black velvet sky. As a child Sarah Jane had lain in bed gazing up at the star-strewn night sky, wondering what might be out there. In her wildest dreams she had never expected to one day find out.

She looked up at them now, and so did Rani.

'Up there, among the stars, and so much further beyond, there are countless fabulous worlds.

There are fantastic civilizations. Life forms beyond our imagination. But there are those that are dangerous. That for whatever reason, mean us harm. I stop them. It's what I do. I've done it for so long.' Sarah Jane paused as she looked at Rani.

Sarah Jane paused. 'But if I could turn back time neither Luke nor Clyde would be involved. I don't know if I'll always be there to protect them.'

She looked at Rani and saw that she was already looking at her, understanding what she was saying: 'You mean you don't need another kid to worry about.'

'No,' Sarah Jane said, 'I don't.'

'But I'm already involved. Odd Bob is coming after me and every other kid that had one of his tickets.'

From her pocket Sarah Jane took a small metal device, and closed Rani's fingers around it. 'This is a Vorgatt defence field emitter. Turn it on and place it in the middle of your room. It will throw up a defence field that will stop anything getting in to harm you. Beyond that, make sure that you are never alone.'

Rani looked at the small gizmo, 'And that's it?'

Sarah Jane took Rani's hands in her own. 'And I promise you that I will stop Spellman.'

Instinctively, Rani knew that Sarah Jane meant it, and – more than that – that she could. Whoever this strange woman really was, whatever had made her into this person, there was something about her that seemed almost invincible.

'If you do stop him, you can't expect me to live across the road and forget all about this.'

'No. But I expect you to keep it a secret. To never tell anyone.'

'Not even Mum and Dad?'

Sarah Jane couldn't help smiling. 'Do you think they would believe you?'

Rani smiled back, shaking her head, 'No.'

Sarah Jane caught that look in Rani's eyes again, the look that in some strange way reminded her so much of herself when she had been that age, 'Goodnight, Rani.'

'Goodnight, Sarah Jane.'

Sarah Jane stood on the pavement and watched Rani head towards her front door. She wanted to be sure that Rani was back in the house with her parents before she headed back to No. 13.

At the door Rani turned back, 'It's amazing isn't it?'

Rani was looking up at the night sky again. 'Aliens and everything. I mean, it's scary. But it's all real and that's...' For a moment, she struggled for the right word, the perfect word... 'That's amazing.'

Sarah Jane felt a burst of warmth inside her. Despite the horrors that Rani had experienced today, what had really touched her were the wonders.

'Yes, Rani. Yes, it is.'

Chapter Nine

The clown in the corner

S arah Jane returned to her house and closed the door behind her, and shuddered. She had told Rani that she would stop Spellman and Odd Bob, and she would if she could. She had lost count of the creatures from other worlds that she had encountered, some of them alone, some of them with the wonderful man she had once travelled the universe with. There had been things that were much more frightening than a clown in a striped costume. The Daleks were terrifying. The Cybermen turned her blood cold.

The Trickster that had literally torn her out of reality had been fearsome. And she had been scared by all of them; fear was natural, and good – it was what sometimes kept you alive. But the terror she had felt this evening in the face of that malevolent clown had been something else entirely. But what had scared her – what scared her now – was that the clown had somehow understood her fear.

Clyde went home shortly after Sarah Jane got back to the house and after a quick supper Luke got ready for bed. Sarah Jane had three rules when it came to mixing home life and dealing with creatures from outer space – that they never discussed aliens at meal times; that they never got in the way of Luke's homework; and that Luke was in bed by ten o'clock before a school day. Things didn't always work out that way, of course, invading aliens rarely factored her son's education into their invasion plans but Sarah Jane thought the principles were worth keeping. Tonight they worked and she kissed Luke goodnight a little before ten.

But Luke wasn't ready to go. He had something on his mind, and she could tell.

'What is it?' Sarah Jane asked.

Luke hesitated. He had seen the look on Sarah

Jane's face as Odd Bob had borne down on her in the museum. And it had haunted him in the hours since.

'Why do clowns scare you so much?'

Sarah Jane looked at him and smiled gently. Her son had been born a teenager. He had never lain in bed at night terrified by his own imagination and the tricks his eyes played in the dark.

Sarah Jane, like every child, knew how that felt. She knew only too well.

She had barely known her parents. They had died in a car crash before her first birthday. For some reason that had never been explained they had left their baby in the care of a neighbour, had gone for a drive and were killed. Sarah Jane had then been brought up by her father's sister, Lavinia.

Professor Lavinia Smith was a virologist with a reputation that spanned the globe. She hadn't married and had never intended to have children, believing she had more important things to do with her life. Motherhood hadn't come naturally or easily to Lavinia when Sarah Jane came under the roof of her rambling Victorian home, but she had loved her in her way and did everything she could for her.

The clown puppet had been one of Lavinia's own toys when she was a girl and she had thought that Sarah Jane would love it. Sarah Jane had, in fact, always hated its creepy smile and its big black eyes but even at the age of five, when Lavinia had given her the precious toy, Sarah Jane didn't want to offend her. And so the marionette hung in a corner in Sarah Jane's bedroom. And every night when she went to bed Sarah Jane would try to avoid its grinning gaze.

And then one night there was a thunderstorm.

Lightning outside the window blasted young Sarah Jane from her sleep. Startled awake, she lay with her ears pounded by the crash of thunder.

Then her eyes found the clown hanging from its strings in the corner, light from the storm outside playing across it.

And Sarah Jane saw its head turn towards her.

And as the thunder struck again she saw it straining against the strings that held it, reaching for her, trying to get at her.

Five-year-old Sarah Jane¯ screamed and screamed.

'I screamed the house down,' Sarah Jane said as she sat on the sofa next to Luke. She smiled when she said it, but she didn't feel like smiling.

'Aunt Lavinia told me not to be so silly. It was a puppet. It was a trick of the light in the storm. And perhaps it was.'

Luke took her hand and squeezed it.

Sarah Jane felt tears in her eyes. 'It was the first time that I ever cried out for my parents.'

Luke could only imagine how that could feel. Sarah Jane may have not given birth to him, but she was all the parent he could ever want. And it was okay for her to get scared once in a while.

Sarah Jane kissed him. She had always believed that an awful lot of Aunt Lavinia had rubbed off on her. Her pragmatism, certainly, and her curiosity and determination as well. And, she had once thought, her attitude towards children. Sarah Jane had once believed she had much more important things to fill her life than children. Luke had shown her just how unlike Aunt Lavinia she truly was. He was the first person other than her aunt that she had told about the clown puppet and she was glad that he was there for her to do so.

The next morning, as she drove out to the Pharos Institute, she felt that telling Luke about the puppet had actually done her good. She had been sure that the encounter with Odd Bob and the animated clown mannequins would bring nightmares of that thunder-struck childhood night to the surface – but she had slept well. And there was nothing like a good night's sleep for going into battle with aliens.

As she left the car and walked up the steps to the doors of the institute she felt good. The feeling lasted all the way up to the polished metal sign that bore its name. That was where she saw Odd Bob's face reflected among the lettering.

Sarah Jane spun around, her nerves instantly drawn tripwire-tight. But there was no sign of the clown.

Sarah Jane shivered in the sunlight and went through the institute's doors. She found Celeste Rivers coming towards her on high heels with a broad smile and an extended hand.

'Miss Smith. So good to see you again,' said Professor Rivers.

The scientist's smile helped Sarah Jane push aside that vision of Odd Bob. Maybe the clown was lurking somewhere, maybe it knew what she was up to. Sarah Jane told herself that it didn't matter – neither Odd Bob, nor Elijah Spellman, or the Pied Piper himself – was going to stop her.

Professor Rivers led Sarah Jane through the

institute explaining that the meteorite that had fallen in the Weserbergland Mountains in the 13th Century had been loaned to Pharos by Munich University.

'Do you know if it's been out of Germany before?' asked Sarah Jane.

'I believe the Americans had it for a time back in the thirties,' said Professor Rivers.

So Luke had been right: Odd Bob had come with the meteor, and had taken children in the States whilst it had been studied there.

Professor Rivers led Sarah Jane into a small laboratory where the meteorite stood on a perspex plinth.

'We've been using the meteorite in experiments in remote viewing with our psychics. Seeing if they can pick up any images of its origin.'

'Oh?' said Sarah Jane. 'With what sort of results?'

'None,' said Professor Rivers flatly. 'None of our psychics will come anywhere near it.'

Sarah Jane raised an eyebrow. She wasn't entirely surprised.

Professor Rivers drew her voice down to little more than a whisper, as if the space rock might hear her. 'It's not dangerous, is it?'

'On the contrary, Professor Rivers, I hope it can

help end something that is.'

The scientist thought it might be better if perhaps she wasn't there while Sarah Jane took her sample from the meteorite. It was, after all, highly irregular. Sarah Jane waited for her to leave and took out the sonic lipstick.

She had promised Professor Rivers that she would hardly notice the difference when she took her sample and Sarah Jane took care in carving off only as much of the space rock as she needed for Mr Smith's analysis. The sonic lipstick sculpted a slice off the meteorite as easily as a knife cutting through butter.

It was then that she heard Spellman's voice.

'What are you doing, Miss Smith?'

Sarah Jane found the ringmaster leaning over her like an inquisitive student. She leaped back in surprise and Spellman's smile grew.

'I didn't mean to frighten you.'

And as if to emphasise just how much of a lie that was, Spellman transformed into the clown before her eyes.

Frightening her was exactly what Spellman wanted to do. But she was determined that he wasn't going to succeed.

'I'm going to find out what you are, Odd Bob,'

she growled. 'We're only scared of what we don't understand. When I know where you come from – what you really are – I will stop you!'

Odd Bob's painted face split into something that looked like a smile but felt like a snarl. 'Is that what you think?'

He took a step towards her, and Sarah Jane couldn't help but shrink back.

'Just suppose there isn't anything to be understood? Suppose I am beyond understanding?'

Sarah Jane felt the palms of her hands turning wet, her throat going dry. Odd Bob took another step towards her, but Sarah Jane refused to move back another foot. She stood there and faced him, and he grinned at her, just inches from her face, his strange silvery eyes boring into hers.

'Suppose, as the thunder crashed and the lightning flashed, your aunt's clown really did come to life?'

Sarah Jane's eyes widened with horror, 'How could you know that?'

But Odd Bob only smiled, delighting in her horror.

'It was a trick of the light,' she gasped.

And then Odd Bob was Spellman again. 'Then why are you still so scared?'

Sarah Jane's jaw tightened with determination. 'I know what you're trying to do. You need people to be frightened of you. That's why you take the children. It's the thing that scares us most, the thing it's almost impossible to understand.'

Spellman's eyes turned hard as flint. 'And today, just for you, Miss Smith, I will chill the blood of a nation. A thousand families will ache with loss and millions will shudder, sleepless with a bone-gnawing fear.'

Sarah Jane yelled at Spellman, 'What are you going to do?'

Behind her the door opened – it was Professor Rivers.

'Are you finished, Miss Smith?'

And Spellman had vanished as if he had never been there.

But he had been there, and he was preparing to do something terrible. The question was, what?

And could she stop him?

Chapter Ten

Red balloons

'The meteorite originated in the Jeggorabax Cluster,' said Mr Smith.

After her confrontation with Spellman and Odd Bob, Sarah Jane had rushed home and straight into the attic. Minutes later Mr Smith had analysed the fragment of meteorite.

'The Jeggorabax Cluster? I've never heard of it.'

Sarah Jane was alone in the attic; Luke, Clyde and Rani were at school.

Mr Smiths said, 'It is a dark nebula on the cusp of the Zeta-Vordak System. Largely unexplored. If I might speak in the modern idiom?'

'If you must.'

'The Jeggorabax Cluster is in the back end of nowhere. In terms of cosmological reference. There are legends about the Jeggorabax Cluster. Unsubstantiated stories from the few craft that have passed through it and survived. Stories of energy entities created by emotion. Particularly fear.'

Sarah Jane absorbed this with interest, sensing that the pieces of the puzzle were falling into place.

'And this energy came here in a meteor that fell near Hamelin where people were terrified by a plague of rats. And their fear manifested as the Pied Piper. Is that possible?'

'Apparently,' said Mr Smith. 'And once manifested the entity required more fear for its survival.'

Sarah Jane grasped what Mr Smith was saying with a chilling horror. 'It took the children. To create fear. And has been doing the same thing ever since.'

That was when Sarah Jane's phone went. She grabbed it.

Luke.

'Mum! I think you'd better get down here!'

It had been break time at Park Vale when the first balloon drifted by.

Luke had been with Clyde and Rani in the playground. It seemed like Rani was coming to terms with the concept of aliens in Ealing, just not with how. And that despite that, life carried on pretty much as always.

'I can't believe we're at school with Odd Bob and Spellman still out there,' she complained.

'Welcome to our world,' Clyde grinned. 'We're the Fearless Alien Hunters, Defenders of Earth – but everything stops for the school bell. Tell me about it!'

But Rani had other things on her mind right now – the red balloon on a string that she had just seen floating by.

'He's here! The balloon – it's Odd Bob! He's here'

Clyde and Luke spun around as Rani pointed – and suddenly there wasn't just one balloon, there were hundreds, drifting in the breeze across the school playground. Other kids had seen them now, and were reaching for the balloons, laughing, jumping and grabbing. But the laughter died as each child took hold of a balloon's string. Their faces froze like masks, and together they started to move.

'It's as if the balloons are taking control of them,' said Luke.

And as a single body, every kid in the school started to move towards and through the school gates.

'He's leading them away,' Rani cried. 'Like the Pied Piper.'

A thousand children being led away.

'Come on,' Clyde called. 'We have to try and stop them.'

They went after the kids into the streets beyond Park Vale, and found themselves swept along in the mass exodus of pupils. Clyde and the others yelled at the blank-faced kids holding the balloons, but none listened. They tried to get in their way, but they walked around them. They tried to hold them back, but they shrugged off their hands. Nothing was going to stop them as they surged along the streets of Ealing – and Luke, Clyde and Rani knew exactly where they were heading.

That's when Luke made his call to Sarah Jane.

'They're heading for the circus museum,' she said as she took his call in the attic and listened to what had happened.

This had to be what Spellman had been talking about in the Pharos laboratory – he was going to make the whole school vanish.

'Luke, whatever you do, don't follow them into the museum,' she said. 'I'll be there as soon as I can.'

She ended the call and turned to leave, but looked at the mobile phone in her hand – she turned back to Mr Smith: she had a job for him.

It didn't take her long to tell the computer what she needed him to do, and ten minutes later she was parking her car outside Spellman's Magical Museum of the Circus as, ahead of her, a sea of schoolchildren headed towards the museum, each clutching a red balloon that swayed in the air above them. She saw Luke, Clyde and Rani running towards her.

'We tried to turn them back, but they just won't listen,' Rani told her.

'Spellman is controlling them like he did the clown mannequins,' Sarah Jane explained. 'He's going to draw them into the museum and they'll disappear like the others.'

'Why?' Clyde demanded. 'Why is he doing it?'

'It isn't the children he's interested in – it's the

fear that their disappearance causes. Spellman is an energy entity that feeds on fear.'

As she spoke Spellman stepped through the museum doors, holding his top hat aloft, calling out to the advancing kids.

'Roll up! Roll up! Welcome to Spellman's Magical Museum of the Circus! There's nowhere like it on Earth – or anywhere else! Just step this way!'

But Sarah Jane stepped between him and the sea of enchanted schoolchildren.

'I don't think so, Mr Spellman.'

He regarded her with cold eyes. 'I don't think you have any say in the matter, Miss Smith.'

Sarah Jane held his gaze, and took out her mobile. 'Perhaps I should call a friend.'

Around them the air was suddenly alive with ring tones. Pop tunes, theme tunes, crazy noises. The street crackled with them. And the kids started letting go of the balloons, and answering their phones, Spellman's control over them broken the same way Rani's phone had broken his control the day before.

'It's Mr Smith,' Luke grinned. 'He's scanned the school records and rung every pupil!'

And as the phones rang, the kids looked around

them confused, and began to move off.

Spellman watched with a face turning dark with rage. 'You meddle with me at your cost, Sarah Jane Smith.'

Sarah Jane enjoyed what she was seeing. 'I'm not scared of you, or Odd Bob. I know what you are. You're an energy entity from the Jeggorabax Cluster. You're the manifestation of a billion moments of fear across seven hundred years. And the scarefest is over – right now!'

Spellman regarded her; his rage had passed and was now replaced with a reptilian cold. 'You think you have conquered your fear, Miss Smith? I will show you fear.'

And Spellman slid backwards through the museum doors, which slammed behind him.

Clyde looked at Rani and Luke and grinned. 'Sounds like a bad loser to me!'

Rani smiled and looked at the kids, they were all moving off now, heading back to school. Spellman had lost.

But instinct told Sarah Jane that Spellman was far from done yet, and when she looked around she felt the blood squeezed out of her heart...

Luke! Where was Luke?

Clyde spun around as Sarah Jane cried out

Luke's name.

'He was right next to me!'

But Luke wasn't there any more.

Luke had vanished.

Sarah Jane felt a wave of nausea surge through her. She had to reach for the wall of the museum to stop herself from falling.

Spellman had Luke. She didn't know how, it didn't matter. She had no doubt. Spellman had taken her son.

Clyde knew it, too, and he was heading for the museum doors, his head down and his face angry. 'No, I'm not having this!'

Sarah Jane caught his arm, 'No Clyde, stay here. You too Rani. I'm going after him on my own.'

'No way,' Clyde protested. 'We're going to help you.'

But Sarah Jane's voice flared, 'I'm not going to risk losing both of you, as well. Now, stay here!'

And she walked through the museum doors. As she did so, she turned, the sonic lipstick in her hands, and locked the doors after her. Clyde and Rani tugged on the doors from the outside, but it was hopeless – Sarah Jane had locked them out.

Chapter Eleven

The day of the clown

Sarah Jane moved slowly through the circus museum, the sonic lipstick held before her. She willed her hands not to shake.

Beside her the mechanical clown in the glass case started to laugh, hyena-like. Sarah Jane spun around and saw it was just the fairground toy. She zapped it with the sonic anyway, and the museum fell into silence.

'Spellman?' she yelled into the silence. 'I've come for my son!'

There was no answer from the museum. Sarah Jane moved on deeper into the museum, passing cautiously between a couple of clown mannequins.

They didn't move, but she couldn't shake the idea that they were watching her.

Through a darkened doorway she suddenly caught movement – it was Luke. It looked as if he was at the far end of another passageway, hammering at a glass wall. He was calling her, but there was no sound.

Sarah Jane ran through the doorway, towards him.

He vanished.

And she found herself surrounded by distorted reflections of herself.

A hall of mirrors.

She spun around, searching for the way she had come in, but all around her seemed to be mirror-lined corridors, all reflecting back weirdly distorted images of herself. Going on instinct, she chose one of the passageways and followed it.

And, ahead of her, there was Odd Bob – his head the size of a tractor tyre, his body thin as a lamp post with no legs, just huge feet.

Another reflection.

The chamber was filled with wild laughter, and then Odd Bob's reflection slipped away.

Sarah Jane spun around, disoriented by the laughter and the mirrors. She screamed into the air, defiant, 'I'm not scared of you!'

Spellman's voice echoed through the hall of mirrors, 'Oh, but I think you are, Miss Smith.'

'If you've hurt my son, Spellman, I will destroy you!'

Spellman chuckled, 'The fear of a mother for her young. The strongest fear of all.'

And Sarah Jane had had enough. 'You had better believe it!'

She aimed the sonic at the nearest mirror, and gave it full power. The mirror shattered into dust. Behind it was a doorway – and Sarah Jane strode through it, ready for battle.

As she did so, Clyde and Rani were in an alleyway at the back of the museum. They had found a half-open window, but Rani was going to need a boost off Clyde if they were going to get through it and help Sarah Jane.

Only Clyde wasn't so sure about Rani going in there. 'Maybe you should stay here. It's going to be dangerous.'

Rani glared at him. 'Would Maria have stayed out here?'

'No,' he admitted. 'But she knew the score. Look, aliens – they've got more tricks up their sleeve than Derren Brown.'

Rani fumed, 'Everything has got to be a joke with you, hasn't it? Can't you just be serious?'

Clyde looked at her, and for a moment Rani barely recognised him. The twinkling light that was always in Clyde's eye had gone. She knew that she hadn't known him long, but she suspected that this was a Clyde that few people knew.

'I've done Serious,' he told her. 'My dad walking out on me and my mum was Serious. I get on better with Funny.'

Rani looked at him, surprised and regretful, 'I'm sorry.'

Clyde shrugged it off and she was relieved to see a smile tugging at the corner of his mouth again. 'Now, you better not put my back out.'

And as Clyde helped Rani through the window, Sarah Jane found herself once more in the clown room surrounded by the lifeless mannequins. She had no doubt that Spellman had in some way manipulated her progress through the museum to bring her here. He knew what scared her but she was determined not to give him what he wanted.

'Come on, Spellman,' she called into the air, 'no more smoke and mirrors. If you're planning on getting fat on my fear, you're looking at a lo-cal lunch!'

But she couldn't help but jump when Odd Bob touched her shoulder from behind. She spun around to face the clown.

He was licking his fingers theatrically, 'Tastes like fear to me.'

'What have you done with Luke?' she demanded, and found she couldn't stop herself backing away from the advancing clown.

'He's with the others,' he said.

'The others?'

Odd Bob started to count them off on his fingers, 'The boy in the stationery store, the boy playing football... if you want me to count them all you should pull up a chair, it has been over seven hundred years, you know.'

'Where are they?'

Odd Bob waved his hands vaguely in the air, 'Somewhere between this world and another. I don't really know where, or what it is. It just is. They're sleeping. I don't want to harm them. I don't need to.'

Sarah Jane's heart fired with hope. 'All of them? They're fine?'

Odd Bob's painted smile turned downwards,

'Well, after a while they just fade away.'

'Bring them back,' she demanded. 'Bring them back now!'

Odd Bob circled her, 'Oh, I can't do that. Can you imagine it? The bogeyman that brings children back from Never-Never-Land? Who would be scared of me then? I would cease... to be.'

As the clown spoke he had changed into Spellman.

Sarah Jane stared at the ringmaster, knowing that she had unlocked the secret to Spellman's existence. 'And if you don't exist any more all the harm you've done is reversed. The children you have taken from here will be returned.'

Spellman snapped his whip against his leg impatiently. 'But you can't destroy me, Miss Smith. No one can destroy fear. It is a part of you all. I am a part of you all.'

The ringmaster took a step towards her. 'Now, if you are so concerned for your son, let me take you to join him. I'm sure that your disappearance will – in time – give me much nourishment.'

Sarah Jane stumbled backwards as Spellman reached for her – and out of the shadows came Clyde...

'Two aerials got married. You should've seen

the reception!'

Spellman and Sarah Jane both turned to look. Both confused.

Clyde was beaming, 'What do you call a sheep with no legs? A cloud!'

Clyde laughed at his own joke, but Spellman was turning on him. 'Another child, another frightened mother. Yes, you have a ticket, Clyde Langer.'

But Clyde slipped away from Spellman, he was moving around the room like a boxer now, firing jokes instead of punches. 'Police station toilet stolen – the cops have nothing to go on!

'What do you call a fish with no eyes? A fsh!'

As Clyde carried on Rani joined Sarah Jane, laughing.

'A magician was driving down the road, then he turned into his house!'

Spellman snarled, 'What is this?'

'Classic material,' Clyde told him. 'What's invisible and smells like carrot? Rabbit farts.'

Sarah Jane laughed. And she knew what Clyde was doing.

'Two snowmen standing in a field – one says to the other, funny I can smell carrots, too!'

Rani chipped in, 'Where would you find a one-legged dog? Where you left him!'

Clyde grinned. 'Hey – she's nicking my material.'

'Stop this!' Spellman spat. 'Stop this now!'

Sarah Jane turned on him. 'What's wrong, Mr Spellman? Does the sound of laughter upset you? Does it frighten you?'

Spellman was starting to shake – it could have been rage, but it could have been something else...

'You will fear me!'

He began to transform into Odd Bob, but failed. He became Spellman again. Sarah Jane felt a thrill run through her body – he was weakening!

Clyde was still hammering out the jokes, 'Optician tells this guy he's colour blind. Well, that's a bolt out of the green! How did Count Dracula get out of Transylvania? He used a blood vessel!'

'People have shuddered with fear in my shadow for seven centuries,' said Spellman.

'And now they're rocking with laughter,' Sarah Jane said. 'That must be a real kick in the ego.'

'I went to the dentist,' said Clyde. 'He said, say ah. I said, why? He said, my dog's died.'

Spellman turned on Sarah Jane with one last burst of malevolence. 'Do you think you can destroy me with these pathetic jokes?'

Clyde looked hurt, 'Hey, these are top-notch gags!'

From her pocket, Sarah Jane took the sliver of meteorite. It glowed in her hand.

'I'm not going to destroy you, Mr Spellman,' she said. 'I'm just going to put you back where you belong.'

Sarah Jane brandished the fragment of meteor and Spellman pulled back a little, afraid.

'This is what brought you to Earth, Spellman. You've always been attached to it, but you were strong enough to resist its pull. But not any more, you're weakening. And now the nightmare is over!'

Sarah Jane thrust the glowing meteor at Spellman.

For a moment Sarah Jane saw the ringmaster's eyes wide with fear. The next instant Spellman's form blew apart into a billion light particles that momentarily tried to reform into the shape of the clown, then seemed to be sucked into the glowing piece of meteorite.

A moment later it was all over. The meteorite's glow faded, became just a rock in Sarah Jane's hand and Spellman had gone.

They could all sense it – the nightmare was

over.

Clyde took a big theatrical bow, 'Thank you! The joker in the pack – every alien-busting team should have one.'

Sarah Jane hugged him. 'Clyde, you were brilliant.'

'Actually, it was Rani's idea. She reckoned laughing was the only way to beat fear.'

Rani grinned, 'Yeah. But I told you to be funny.'

Then, out of the darkness came Luke, 'Mum?'

Sarah Jane could barely contain her joy as she threw her arms around him. 'Luke! Are you all right?'

'I'm fine. What happened? Where's Spellman.'

She held him tightly and smiled, 'I imagine you could say he finally paid the piper.'

Chapter Twelve

The secret

Rani watched as Sarah Jane placed the fragment of meteorite in a small metal box. They were back in the attic now and Mr Smith had told them that Dave Finney and the other kids that had disappeared had all been found safe and sound. None had any idea of where they had been, or any memory of the clown. It was a mystery that would never be solved. The metal box was something called Halkonite steel, Sarah Jane had said – nothing could get through it, not even thought. That was the last they were ever going to see of the Pied Piper – except in fairytales.

'And stuff like this – it happens to you all the time?' Rani asked.

'You get used to it,' Clyde said, and flashed her a smile. 'Weird happens.'

'Of course, not all aliens are bad,' said Sarah Jane.

'Just the ones that come here,' said Clyde. 'It's like Earth has this big sign in orbit – Invade Please!'

Sarah Jane put the Halkonite steel box in a cupboard and scolded playfully, 'Clyde, you know that's not true. There are lots of good, decent aliens.'

'But they do tend to stay at home watching TV,' Luke grinned.

Rani burst out laughing and Luke's jaw dropped with joy. 'She laughed! She likes my jokes!'

But Rani stopped laughing when she noticed Sarah Jane watching her.

'So what happens now,' she asked. 'Do you trust me to keep all this secret?'

Sarah Jane seemed to be thinking carefully as she crossed the attic, watched by Luke and Clyde just as closely as by Rani, all three wondering what she would say.

'When it comes to getting a true glimpse of the universe, there are two types of people,' she said. 'Those who refuse to believe, that will tell themselves anything to deny the evidence of their eyes, to keep themselves safe in their tiny world.

And those who embrace the universe, and just how special life is, and that want to keep it that way, by keeping it safe and secret.'

'And that's me?' Rani asked hopefully.

Sarah Jane smiled and gathered Luke, Clyde and Rani in her arms, and gazed out of the attic window towards the darkening evening sky.

'That's all of us,' she said.